BABE
The Sheep Pig™

Looking for Dash

By Molly Kates • Illustrated by Jan Gerardi

Random House 🏠 New York

Library of Congress Catalog Card Number: 98-65564 ISBN 0-679-89192-7 (trade) ; 0-679-99192-1 (lib. bdg.)
www.randomhouse.com/kids/
Printed in the United States of America 10 9 8 7 6 5 4 3 2 1
JELLYBEAN BOOKS is a trademark of Random House, Inc.

One day on Hoggett's farm, Fly noticed
that one of her puppies was missing.
"Where could Dash be?" she wondered.
"I'll find him!" said Babe.

Babe looked in the barn. There was no puppy.
But there were three mice. The mice said they'd
help Babe look for Dash.

Babe and the mice looked in the chicken coop.

There was no puppy. But there were a bunch
of chickens, one rooster, and Ferdinand the duck.
Ferdinand wanted to help look for Dash, too.

Babe, the mice, and Ferdinand trooped
to the fields.
"Have you seen a puppy?" Babe asked
the sheep.

"No little wolves here," the sheep baa-ed.
"He's not a wolf," Babe said. "He's a little puppy."
But the sheep hadn't seen a little puppy either.

"Let's sit down and think," Babe said to his team.

"I don't know why I'm here," Ferdinand quacked.

"Because we all need to help each other," said Babe. "Dash may be lost *and* hungry *and* scared."

"Oh, where, oh, where has that little dog gone?" sang the first mouse.

"Right *there!*" shrieked the second mouse, jumping up and down with excitement.

Babe looked. And sure enough, over at the edge of the woods, he spotted a flash of black and white.

"Come on, you guys!" cried Babe. "Let's go get him!"

The animals all charged across the fields.

Into the shadows under the trees they ran,
quacking, oinking, and squealing Dash's name.
Then they stopped short. There in front of them

was a furry black-and-white animal. But it wasn't
Dash—it was a *very* surprised skunk!

Just then a giggle came from behind a tree.

"Here I am!" cried Dash, and out he jumped.
At that very moment, the skunk lifted her tail
and let loose.

"Pee-yew!" everybody cried.
"So sorry," said the skunk.
"But you surprised me."

"Poor Dash," laughed Babe. "What you need is a bath in tomato juice."

"Yum, yum, yum!" sang the mice.